How to Catch a Falling Star

Written by Heidi Howarth
Illustrated by Daniel Howarth

QEB
QEB Publishing

"What are you doing?" asked Hedgehog.

"Sitting and waiting for the star to fall," replied Bear grumpily. "The last star of the year."

"Oh. Can I wait, too?"

Bear said nothing. He just shuffled along to make a space.

And they sat and waited.

"What are you doing?" asked Mouse.

"Sitting and waiting for that star to fall," replied Hedgehog and Bear, pointing high up into the treetop.

"Oh. Can Rabbit and I wait, too?"

Bear and Hedgehog said nothing. They just shuffled along to make a space.

And they sat and waited.

Squirrel had been watching
from high in the treetops.
He had a wonderful idea.

"Don't worry, I can get it
down for you," he called.

He reached out his paw...

"No!" cried Bear, Hedgehog, and Mouse.

Rabbit was too shy and said nothing.

"Don't touch it!" said Bear. "If you touch it, the magic will be lost."

Squirrel stopped.

"What magic?"

"Very strong magic, but not if you touch it!" shouted Bear.

Squirrel looked closely. The leaf looked the same as all the other leaves he had seen on the tree.

Squirrel scampered down the tree and rummaged through a pile of leaves.

"What is he doing?" asked Bear.

"I can't see," said Mouse. "I'm too small."

Bear smiled for the first time.
"Sit on my shoulder if you like."

Mouse was surprised.
"Thank you," he said.

No one noticed Squirrel
scampering back up the
tree. Now he sat there
with a leaf in his hand.

Silently,
he dropped it.

Bear gasped, Hedgehog shook,
Mouse squeaked, and they all
watched the leaf fall.

"We have to catch it,"
called Bear.

"We have to catch
the magic."

But where had it gone?

Still, no one had noticed Squirrel.
Suddenly his little tummy shook
as he let out a big chuckle.

They all looked up.

"It's right there," chuckled Squirrel.

"Behind you!"

Bear turned around, but the leaf wasn't there.

Mouse and Rabbit turned around, but the leaf wasn't there.

Hedgehog turned around, but he couldn't see the leaf either.

Suddenly Bear, Rabbit, and Mouse started to laugh.

"The leaf's not behind you. It's on your behind!" they cried, pointing to the leaf on Hedgehog's prickles.

"What's wrong?" asked Hedgehog.

"The magic is gone, and I needed it," cried Bear.

"But what for?" asked Mouse.

"To wish for someone to play with." Bear started to cry.

...at all? You have us, silly!"

cried Hedgehog, Mouse, Squirrel,

and even Rabbit.

And with that, the five friends
played together every day.

The magic of the leaf had worked.

Notes for parents and teachers

- Look at the front cover of the book together. Can the children guess what the story might be about? Read the title together. Does this give them more of a clue?

- When the children first read the story, or you read it together, can they guess what might happen at the end? Do they think Bear believes it is a real star? Could he really catch a star?

- What other things can the children name that are star-shaped? Ask them to draw pictures of the items.

- Leaves come in all different shapes and sizes, as well as different colors. Do the children know what happens to leaves before winter? Discuss the changing seasons. Can the children name all the seasons? Which is their favorite?

- For a group activity, you could go for a walk with the children, even around the yard. There, you will find lots of different leaves and small creatures.

- You could make a story (journey) stick. To do this, give each child a twig. Then you all go on a little walk and collect objects. This could be a leaf, feather, or flower. Each item is attached to the stick with a piece of string or tape, in the order they are found. Once you return home or back to school, ask the children to tell a story from the items they have found. Children will get wonderful ideas and enjoy showing their collections to other children.

- Another strong theme in this book is friendship. What makes a good friend? What is fun about having friends? You could discuss which games they like to play together.

Copyright © QEB Publishing, Inc. 2010

Published in the United States by
QEB Publishing, Inc.
3 Wrigley, Suite A
Irvine, CA 92628

www.qed-publishing.co.uk

ISBN 978-1-84835-368-8

Printed in China

Editor: Amanda Askew
Designers: Vida and Luke Kelly

A CIP record for this book is available from the Library of Congress.